Cover design by Elaine Lopez-Levine.

Little, Brown and Company

Hachette Book Group
1290 Avenue of the Americas, New York, NY 10104
Visit us at lb-kids.com
Visit monsterhigh.com

First Edition: February 2017

Little, Brown and Company is a division of Hachette Book Group, Inc. The Little, Brown name and logo are trademarks of Hachette Book Group, Inc.

The publisher is not responsible for websites (or their content) that are not owned by the publisher.

Library of Congress Control Number 2016958379

ISBNs: 978-0-316-54826-7 (hardcover), 978-0-316-54836-6 (pbk.), 978-0-316-54833-5 (ebook)

10 9 8 7 6 5 4 3 2 1

LSC-C

Printed in the United States of America

MONSTER HIGH
ELECTRIFIED

The Junior Novel

BY
Perdita Finn

BASED ON THE SCREENPLAY BY
KEITH WAGNER

LITTLE, BROWN AND COMPANY
New York   Boston

Chapter 1

GHOULS OFF THE GRID

The moon was full in the sky. Bugs whirred. A cricket chirped. A wolf howled. *"Awoo! Awoo!"* But it was not a happy sound. It was a cry of distress. The wolf was in terrible trouble.

The wolf bounded down the empty street of the town. She looked over her shoulder. She was exhausted from running, but the mob of Normies was still after her. The moon was so bright; there was nowhere for the wolf to hide. She ran along the sidewalk close to a building, trying to stay in the shadows. How much longer could she run?

She could hear the angry voices of the mob.

They were hunting her because she was different. Because she was a monster.

She turned a corner, hoping to catch her breath, but someone was right in front of her, ready to trap her! The wolf bounded forward as fast as she could, dodging past legs and hands that reached out to grab her fur. She took off like lightning down the street.

"It went that way!"

"Did you see it?"

"Don't lose it!"

She couldn't stop. She had to keep going. She dashed into a dark alley, but it dead-ended in a chain-link fence. In a single bound, she leaped over the fence, turning a somersault in midair—and in an instant she began to transform. Her claws turned into fingernails, her paws into hands, her snout into the nose of a teenage ghoul. When she landed on the other side of the fence, she wasn't a wolf anymore; she was a weregirl.

The ghoul's long mane of blue hair was streaked with purple and lighter blue and was held back in a thick ponytail. She wore a purple tank top and a stylish skirt with black heels. She was exhausted from running, but that didn't matter; she couldn't stop. She had to get away from the mob!

The glare of their flashlights brightened the alley. She tried not to breathe too loudly as she peeked around the corner to see what they were up to.

"It's here somewhere…" she heard someone saying.

She was trying to stay absolutely still, but her foot slipped and landed on an empty can.

"Did you hear that?" asked a boy's voice.

All the flashlights focused on a pile of boxes in the alley.

"There!" shouted someone in the mob. A beam of light shone in her eyes for an instant before she was off again.

She ran as fast as she could.

She checked behind her. No one had caught up with her yet.

The angry shouts of the mob were coming closer. She clambered up a wall and ran along the roof of a high building, but it was another dead end. There was an even bigger wall in front of her. There was nowhere else to go.

"Have you seen it?"

"Where could it have gone?"

The mob was just below her.

"Maybe it climbed the fence," someone wondered.

"Nah, wolves can't climb. Let's check the other side."

The weregirl had been holding her breath, hugging the shadows. But before she could relax, a giant orb of light flashed before her. It had come out of nowhere!

She rubbed her eyes. She blinked. Standing in front of her was a group of five ghouls. Bright, welcoming smiles flashed across their faces, but the weregirl didn't wait to find out if they were friendly. She leaped back down into the alley.

She didn't hear their warm words of greeting. She didn't notice their fangtastic fashions. She didn't realize that one of the ghouls had sharp canine teeth and furry ears poking out from among the brown curls of her thick hair...just like she had when she wasn't a wolf.

"Hi, we're your welcoming committee, and we would just like to say..." began Draculaura, the ghoul with jet-black hair streaked with pink. She was a vampire but a devoted vegetarian. "Uh, where is she?"

"Down here!" The weregirl blinked up at them. Who were they? Could they help her? Maybe they could! "Help me, please! They've got the place surrounded!" She spoke with a thick Scottish accent.

"Did you hear that?"

"Over there!"

The mob was circling back toward the alley!

Clawdeen Wolf, who was also a werewolf, noticed the crowd and shook her head. "So rude!"

"I think we'd better do something," Frankie Stein suggested. The daughter of Frankenstein, she had two gleaming bolts poking out from either side of her neck.

"Of course," agreed Cleo de Nile, the mummy princess. "But will we still have time for a bite…"

"I see something!" shouted a man in the mob.

"Ghouls! Let's move!" Clawdeen urged.

The ghouls sprang into action. There was no time to lose. Frankie spotted an electrical box on the side of the building and zapped it with a sizzling bolt from her fingertips. All the floodlights in the neighborhood blinked and blitzed. Everything became dark.

"Whoa!" shouted someone down below. "Is there a blackout?"

"What's going on?"

Meanwhile, Draculaura turned herself into a bat and dove toward the crowd in the dark. People covered their heads, shrieking.

"Ahhh!"

"What was that?"

Cleo whistled sharply, getting the weregirl's attention. She dropped down a long mummy bandage for her to climb to safety.

"There!" shouted someone, spotting her as she scampered upward.

"Don't let it get away!"

Together, the ghouls hoisted the weregirl onto the top of the building.

"Oh, thank you," the weregirl said once she was finally safe.

"No worries." Lagoona Blue smiled. The daughter of a sea monster, Lagoona was very friendly.

"No problem," added Cleo.

Frankie grinned. "Our pleasure."

"Happy to help," said Draculaura.

"It's what we do!" Clawdeen was thrilled to meet another monster just like her.

The weregirl looked at all the friendly ghouls in front of her. She'd never seen anyone like them. She'd never seen anyone like *her*. "Who are you?"

Draculaura took this as her cue to finally deliver the speech she gave to all prospective Monster High students. "Hi, we're your official welcoming committee, and we would just like to say—"

But shouting from below interrupted Draculaura's introduction. The mob was angrier than ever.

"It circled back! Bust down the gate!"

"I'll get the truck! Someone get the lights back on!"

"Where's the ladder?"

"Boost me up, guys!"

Clawdeen was worried. "Uh, ghouls? I think the Normies figured out that they've been tricked. Time to go!"

Frankie pulled out the small glowing Skullette. The ghouls used it for transport when they were recruiting new students. It let them travel all over the world to find monsters in hiding everywhere. They all placed their hands on it—except for the new ghoul.

"Don't worry," Frankie reassured her. "We're monsters too, obviously. Come on!"

The weregirl added her hand to the Skullette... and with a blast...and a flash...and a whoosh, they all disappeared in an instant from the roof.

Suddenly, they were standing in front of an ancient castle. Huge steps led up to the front door of the building, which was surrounded protectively by high mountains. Monsters of all kinds were going in and out of the castle, books in their hands. At last Draculaura could finish her speech!

All her friends crowded around the new ghoul.

"Okay!" Draculaura sighed with relief. "So, as your official welcoming committee, we would just like to say..."

"Welcome to Monster High!" everyone chimed in all together.

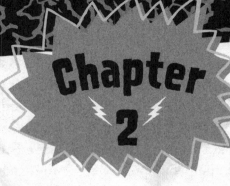

Chapter 2

SPARKS FLY

Monster High was a top secret school for monsters of all kinds. Before Frankie Stein and Draculaura met, they hadn't known that there were other monsters in the world—other monsters who were lonely, just like they had been. They decided that they would create a special school for all the beasties, boogeys, and not-so-mythical banshees they could find. They were the first students, but soon they were finding mummy princesses like Cleo. They traveled to Greece to recruit the snake-haired son of a gorgon, and to Australia to find a surfing sea monster. The first weregirl they found was Clawdeen, who came to Monster High with all her werepup brothers and even her mom, who was now the art teacher.

At Monster High, the students accepted one another's differences and learned about the monster world together. They even learned about the Normies, the people who weren't monsters, so that maybe one day they would all know how to get along and monsters could come out of hiding. That was Draculaura's and Frankie's biggest dream.

The day after the new weregirl, Silvi Timberwolf, arrived, they were all sitting in science class together. Frankie had on goggles. She was watching very carefully as a frizzling zap of pure electricity arced between her fingers. She was using it to weld together two pieces of metal. *Zap!* Sparks flew into the air.

All around the room, monsters were working on experiments.

Rayth, a musician, carefully poured a test tube of bubbling liquid into a beaker. Gob, his purple blob monster of a partner, watched cheerfully. But then Gob got hungry and ate their experiment.

Lagoona was reading directions while Cleo added another ingredient to the plant they were cultivating. Uh-oh. Its leaves withered. Lagoona looked across the room.

Frankie was carefully adjusting a fixture on her project. Clawdeen handed her tools without looking up from her sketchpad. She was working on some new fashions that were experimental in their own way, if not exactly scientific!

"Frankie is really amped up about this project," Lagoona noted.

Draculaura looked over at her friend, impressed. "Have you seen it? It's a… It's… amazing! Isn't it?"

Clawdeen, continuing with her sketching, smiled. "You have no idea what it is, do you?"

"Nope," admitted Draculaura.

"Glad I'm not the only one!" Lagoona added.

"No idea," agreed Clawdeen.

"What is that thing anyway?" Cleo wondered out loud.

Frankie stopped working and raised her goggles. Wires spewed messily from the small metal object. It looked like some kind of battery.

"It's an ultra-high-density direct-current capacitor for storing high levels of electrical energy."

The ghouls glanced at one another, baffled.

Cleo smiled politely. "Neat."

"It's like a super battery." Frankie laughed. "I'm trying to put all that electricity"—she pointed overhead at huge coils—"into this! Imagine having to charge your phone only once a year! Oh, and for the Normies, electricity is everything. This device is really going to change their world for the better."

Frankie hoped that if a monster invented something that helped the Normies, they might come to accept the monsters.

"Amazing!" exclaimed Draculaura, who finally understood.

"Fascinating," Cleo added, genuinely curious.

Lagoona grinned. "Ace!"

But not everyone was impressed.

"Why would you want to help Normies? They've never tried to help us." Moanica D'Kay sneered. The zombie was slouched against the back wall of the lab, one of her Zomboy minions standing on either side of her. They were dressed in khakis and button-downs. They kind of looked like prep-school students, but they gazed up at the ceiling, their mouths open, drooling a little bit.

Moanica sauntered over to Frankie's table to get a good look at her project. She shoved Gob out of her way. Moanica began fiddling with the experiment. She pulled on wires and tipped it upside down. "How do you work this thing anyway?"

The Zomboyz laughed obediently.

"Moanica, don't touch that," begged Frankie. "It's not—"

But Moanica never listened to anybody. She flicked a switch, and electricity sizzled from the giant coils into Frankie's device. A flash exploded in the lab!

"Whoa!"

"Yikes!"

"No!"

The room was completely dark. Moanica was shocked—literally! Her mane of silvery hair was standing completely on end. With a shiver, she pulled herself together.

"It's not done yet." Frankie sighed.

Moanica didn't care. She sauntered out of the room with her frazzled Zomboyz. Those ghouls annoyed her, but they had given her an idea. A terrible idea. A wicked smile turned up the corners of her mouth. She slammed the door behind her as she left.

The room crackled with energy; bolts shot from the sizzling coils.

Chapter 3

MAKING CONNECTIONS

Outside, the wind was blowing, and lightning flashed across the sky. Swirls of leaves careened through the air. An adult werewolf with a jaunty scarf around her neck was looking at one of the high-up castle windows. It was Clawdeen's mother, who worked at Monster High. She was holding a large armful of wooden boards. She glanced up again at the window with concern.

Dracula was perched on a narrow window ledge. He was holding nails in his mouth and hammering boards over the windows in preparation for the coming storm.

"Will you get down from there?"

Clawdeen's mom scolded him. "You're making me incredibly nervous." The stormy winds were picking up.

"I appreciate your concern," answered Dracula in his thick accent, continuing to hammer. "But the weather-human says that this is going to be the storm of the century!"

He gestured with his hands and nearly fell backward.

Clawdeen's mom did not look reassured. "Well, watch your step up there! You're going to fall!"

"Ha!" He laughed. "I've been taking care of myself for hundreds of years. I am not going to—"

His foot slipped. The other foot slipped. For a moment, he was bicycling both his feet in the air. The board he was holding spun out of his arms. *Crash!* Down, down, down he plummeted—right into Mrs. Wolf's arms. She caught him effortlessly.

She raised an eyebrow and he was a little bit embarrassed—but only for an instant.

Dracula brushed a dark lock of hair from his eyes. "I did that on purpose," he said coolly. "Thank you."

Clawdeen's mom laughed. She wasn't fooled.

"Sure you did."

In an instant, Dracula transformed himself into a bat. He grabbed a hammer in his claws and, struggling with the weight of it, slowly fluttered back up toward the window. Mrs. Wolf watched him, shaking her head. Thunder rumbled in the distance.

The end-of-class bell rang, and students filled the hallways of Monster High. They were headed to their coffin-shaped lockers and then to the Creepeteria for lunch and Mummy Mochas.

"How was Humanology?"

"I have fearleading today!"

"Wanna play Casketball later?"

From the top of the stairs, Frankie looked down at the happy, chattering students. "Isn't this great?" she said to Draculaura. "Just look at all these monsters. Together under one roof, making friends with one another."

Lagoona sped by on her skateboard. Bonesy was trying to imitate her, but he fell off his board, and his skull rolled across the floor. He chased after it and stuck it back on his skeleton. Deuce Gorgon, the boy whose hair was made of hissing snakes, fist-bumped his buddy Gob.

"Looking good, Gob," he said. But his fist went right through Gob's rolls of goo and got stuck. He tried to pull out his hand, but he couldn't. Gob wiggled back and forth along the hall until his goo could pop free.

Silvi, the new weregirl, was settling right in. She was using a giant paint roller to decorate Woolee's fingernails. They sparkled with a rainbow of pretty colors. Woolee gave her a mammoth hug when she was done.

"It looks like our new ghoul has made a friend," Frankie noted happily.

The ghoulfriends headed outside together. The storm was coming closer. The sky was getting grayer and grayer. Lightning flashed in the distance. The wind was beginning to blow forcefully.

Draculaura was reminiscing. "It's hard to believe that just a few short months ago, Monster High didn't even exist."

"Yeah," agreed Frankie. "It's strange to think that just last year I was hiding with Pops. I'd never even seen another monster. Now I can't take two steps without bumping into—"

Just as she said that, Frankie tripped over a ghoul's legs. The ghoul was sitting on the steps that led up to the main entrance hall. She was all by herself, quietly reading a book.

The shy ghoul had a fringe of streaked blue bangs and shoulder-length hair. But something about her outfit and mysterious expression made her seem to disappear in the shadows or blend in to the stonework—even in broad daylight.

"Oh my ghoul, I am so sorry! I didn't see you there!" Frankie apologized. She felt terrible.

The ghoul shrugged. "Yeah, I get that a lot. When you're the daughter of the Boogey Man, you kind of, well, fade into the shadows."

Draculaura gave the ghoul a friendly smile. "You're Twyla, right? What are you doing here all alone?"

"I like to hang out here during lunch." But she didn't meet Draculaura's eyes when she spoke.

"All by yourself?" Frankie questioned. She was always on the lookout for monsters who needed a friend.

"Sure," said Twyla softly. Her voice was like the

creak of a door in the middle of the night. "I like my alone time," she added.

Draculaura grinned. "Hey, I like alone time too. Come with us and we'll be alone together." She linked her arm around Twyla's and headed toward the courtyard with her.

Music was booming. Ari Hauntington was letting loose and singing her heart out. In the Normie world, Ari was a pop sensation known as Tash, but here at Monster High she could be her spectral self…which was a ghost. Still, ghost or Normie, she was always singing!

Monsters cheered as Ari belted out one of her top hits.

"We love you!"

"Sing it, ghoul!"

Twyla was nervous. She wasn't used to being around so many people.

"You can always be alone at an Ari concert," shouted Draculaura, trying to reassure her. "Alone with the music!" She and Frankie waved their hands to the beat.

Monsters were singing along and dancing. Twyla looked overwhelmed by it all.

"I used to travel the world, performing song after song, but now I'm here at Monster High, right where I belong!" Ari sang. Her long purple hair fell in curls to her waist. She seemed to sing even better when she was just being herself.

The ghouls cheered. "Isn't Ari just creeperific?" Draculaura asked Twyla.

But Twyla was already gone. She had vanished into the shadows.

"Guess she's not a music fan," said Draculaura.

"Maybe she's just shy," Frankie explained.

"*Oooh*, I feel terrible. We should throw her a party to apologize. Like a really big party, and invite the whole school—" Draculaura's imagination was running away with her. She was getting very excited.

"Yeah," interrupted Frankie. "Maybe hold off on those invitations, Draculaura."

Meanwhile, Deuce was rocking out to the music with his friend Rayth. "Man, wonder what it's like to be up onstage like that?" he thought out loud.

"Deuce!" shouted Rayth, getting a great idea. "We should totally start our own band!"

"Yes! Yes!" Deuce pumped his fist in the air. "I am liking this idea."

Rayth turned to the skeletons dancing beside them. "Bonesy? Skelly? You in?"

They started wailing on air guitars. They were psyched!

"That's the spirit!" exclaimed Rayth.

Silvi and Woolee and their friend Venus McFlytrap overheard the boys.

"I play a lot of instruments," Silvi told Rayth.

"And I've loved music ever since I was a

seedling," added Venus. The daughter of the plant monster had a punk-rock look: one half of her head shaved, the other half a pink mane.

Woolee, who didn't talk a lot, nudged Silvi.

"And Woolee too!" Silvi said to the boys.

"Depends," answered Rayth. "Can you ghouls do this?" He played some more air guitar, making all kinds of electronic noises.

The ghouls laughed and began strumming imaginary guitars too.

Deuce was impressed. "Wow! You're good!"

"You are in!" Rayth shouted.

They all started air-jamming together—while the real music came from Ari singing on the stage.

No one noticed that overhead, the clouds were becoming thicker and darker. The storm was getting closer. Lightning flashed.

Chapter 4

A LIVE WIRE

Dracula was in the front of the classroom teaching his favorite subject—Humanology. Students were listening attentively. Clawdeen was doodling in her notebook. Webby, Draculaura's pet spider, was sitting on the top of Dracula's desk.

Dracula gestured toward Webby. "But while all of us monsters find spiders like Webby here to be charming and wonderful creatures…"

Webby blushed modestly and covered his face with one of his legs.

Dracula continued his lecture. "Still, it is important to remember that whenever humans see a spider, they do this…"

Dracula dramatically cleared his throat before demonstrating the usual human reaction to seeing a spider. He freaked out. He screamed, he ran around in circles, he waved his hands over his head. *"AHHHHHHH!"*

The students watched thoughtfully and took careful notes. They couldn't believe it. How could anyone be frightened of Webby? Human beings were so strange.

Dracula stopped and composed himself. He smoothed his hair back into place. "Any questions?"

Deuce was scribbling away as fast as he could. He read over his notes. "*Ahhhh.* Got it."

"Very good." Dracula said, nodding. "Then we're moving on to our next Humanology subject." He walked across the room and flicked off the light switch. "Darkness!"

Dracula turned the light back on. "Now, who can tell me what human beings think about the dark?"

Hands flew up in the air.

"I know! I know!" called Draculaura, jumping up and down in her seat.

"Oh yeah! Yeah!" Even Webby knew the answer.

Dracula surveyed the room of eager students. There was only one who didn't have her hand up. "Clawdeen Wolf?"

Clawdeen blinked. She stammered. She was caught off guard. She hadn't been paying attention. At all. She looked up from her sketch pad. "Huh? Oh—um—they think it's clawesome? Because it is?"

"Absolutely wrong." Dracula shook his head. "Humans are scared of the dark."

The class burst out laughing. Moanica, who was sitting back in her seat with her feet up on her desk, snickered. How could humans be afraid of the dark?

"What's to be scared of?" said Venus out loud. She was genuinely curious.

"Look out! There's some darkness behind you!" Deuce guffawed. *"Ahhh!"*

Dracula waited a moment for the monsters to settle down. "Yes, yes, I know it's peculiar, but it's true. Humans cannot see in the dark like vampires and werewolves."

Moanica, who had been disinterested until

now, leaned forward in her seat. "Normies are afraid of the dark..." she said to herself. Her brow was furrowed. She was thinking hard. "Now that is interesting."

Rayth raised his hand. "Professor Dracula? If the humans are so scared, why don't they just suck up a lightbulb like Gob?"

With that as a cue, Gob produced a lightbulb and gobbled it up. His whole blobby body glowed! The class burst out laughing—except for Draculaura.

"Listen up," she told her friends. "You mansters and ghouls need to take this seriously. We must learn about humans so that one day we can live together happily."

"Ha!" Moanica stood up in the back of the room. The Zomboyz followed her reluctantly— they were her minions, after all, and they were obedient. "I say we should learn about Normies so that we can get back at them for making us hide in the first place." She put her hand on her hip defiantly.

"Moanica," Dracula reprimanded her. "Please take your seat so that we can continue the lecture."

But she ignored the teacher. "I've already heard plenty, Professor Dracula." She rudely examined her fingernails, not even looking him in the eye. "And thank you for the lesson," she said, a hint of sarcasm in her voice. "It was...enlightening." She strode right past Dracula and headed toward the classroom door. Embarrassed, the Zomboyz staggered after her.

As she exited, she clicked off the lights, and the whole room went dark. Except for the green glow from Gob's stomach.

"Whoa!"

"What's going on?"

"Is class over?" someone whispered.

"No!" answered Dracula, confused. Why had Moanica left? What a strange student she was, even for a monster!

Chapter 5

WATT'S UP?

Moanica sauntered down the hallway, flanked by a couple of hollow-eyed Zomboyz. Their green shirts matched the green streak in her hair. She was up to something!

"I just got an idea!" she whispered to the Zomboyz.

She lurked in the doorway of the art room. Clawdeen's mom was instructing a group of monsters in painting. A couple of Zomboyz were in the back of the room dabbing at canvasses with their paintbrushes. Moanica motioned for them to follow her, and they did. Mrs. Wolf was surprised. There had never been a student this disrespectful at Monster High!

Moanica marched from classroom to classroom, from the reception desk to the Creepeteria, collecting her army of obedient Zomboyz. The moment she snapped her fingers, they put down their lunch trays and followed her.

In the library, they frightened away all the other students by blasting music on giant loudspeakers. Moanica pointed here and there. She directed the Zomboyz to begin collecting books. They brought her stacks and stacks of them—all about electricity. They staggered under huge, toppling towers of books.

Moanica sat in a rolling chair, and they pushed her up and down the aisles so she could look for exactly what she wanted. She tossed books over her shoulder, and the Zomboyz caught them.

In a shadowy corner of the library, a ghoul peeked over the top of her book. It was Twyla! At first, she was annoyed by all the noise, but then she became suspicious. What was Moanica up to?

Moanica had spread out a map on one of the tables. She was studying it. She spotted something and a big grin spread across her face.

Her next stop was the Mad Science lab. The classroom was empty when she went in. Experiments and projects were spread out across desks and tables. But the first thing that caught Moanica's eye was Frankie's special battery. She was about to pick it up to examine it when she stopped. Was it dangerous? Maybe. She motioned to a Zomboy to get it for her.

Zap! The Zomboy's fingers touched the battery and he flew backward, jolted by a blast of electricity.

Moanica smiled. This was exactly what she was looking for.

Frankie was coming into the lab to do some more work on her project when she spotted Moanica and the Zomboyz. What were they doing in there? She stepped backward into the shadows before they saw her. They were up to something. But what?

With a gleeful smirk on her face, Moanica sailed past Frankie down the hallway, followed by her Zombovz. Frankie watched them. It was never a good sign when Moanica and the Zomboyz gathered together like that, and Frankie was worried they might be up to trouble.

Moanica was ordering the Zomboyz around.
She handed a pile of books to one boy. "You, read
all these. You, gather some of these," she said to
another. "You, get me a Mummy Mocha!"

Twyla appeared beside Frankie. "What do you
think they're up to?"

"I don't know...Wait, who said that?"

Twyla emerged from the shadows. "Hey, you
want me to keep an eye on those Zomboyz for
you? I could see what they're planning."

Frankie thought about it. "As class president,
this is my responsibility. But thank—"

But Twyla had vanished into thin air! She
wasn't there anymore.

"Twyla?" Frankie called as she looked around,
confused.

Twyla moved ever so slightly. She was right
in front of Frankie, and Frankie hadn't even
seen her!

Frankie jumped, startled. "*Gah!* Okay, you are
really good at that."

Twyla shrugged shyly, secretly pleased by
Frankie's compliment. When your main talent is

disappearing, most people don't really notice it.

Frankie was thinking. "Maybe you *should* keep an eye on them. But you let me know as soon as you find anything. Whatever she's up to, I'll deal with it."

Twyla nodded.

"I've got a feeling something big is on the horizon," Frankie mused.

A huge boom interrupted her thoughts. Both Frankie and Twyla jumped this time.

"Was that thunder?" exclaimed Frankie.

Just then they spotted a cymbal careening down the stairwell. Embarrassed laughter followed close behind. "Sorry," apologized Deuce. He pointed at the instruments rolling in front of him as he ran to catch them. "Runaway drum kit."

"We're starting a band!" Rayth explained. He held his bass over his head.

Silvi, Venus, and Woolee traipsed past them carrying guitars and triangles and bongos.

Twyla's eyes met Frankie's, and they both laughed.

Frankie raised an eyebrow. They had bigger problems to deal with!

Chapter 6

LIGHTNING BOLT!

Thunder boomed. Lightning flashed, cutting jagged stitches in the sky. Rain pelted down on Monster High. The storm had begun. Werewolf pups howled throughout the castle.

Frankie looked out the window of the tower room where the ghouls were hanging out. She was thinking about her battery project and all that electrical energy loose in the world. She could just see the hulking shadow of the town's abandoned power station off in the distance—the same power station she'd hid in not so long ago. It harnessed energy. How could she do the same thing with her battery?

The other ghouls were lounging around in the loft together telling scary stories. They'd finished their drinks and their snacks. They were in a cozy circle. Clawdeen hugged a fluffy pillow. Cleo leaned in, captivated. Ari held up a flashlight to her face to make it spookier as she told her story. "And she heard a noise," she continued breathlessly. "As she was walking down a dark tunnel, what she saw wasn't a ghost at all. It… was…a…HUMAN!"

The ghouls gasped and shivered, terrified. Webby shrieked and leaped into the air, his legs flying in eight different directions.

"*Aahhhh!*" screeched Clawdeen. Then she burst out laughing with relief. A human. That was all. That didn't have to be so frightening.

"You got me!" Cleo laughed, catching her breath.

"That was really scary," Lagoona agreed. Her eyes were still wide.

Clawdeen noticed Frankie by the window. "Come on," she called to her. "Let's play Truth or Scare!"

Frankie grabbed a pillow and joined her

friends. This was one of her favorite games.

"Okay, Truth or Scare," she began. "Um...." She looked around the circle of her ghoulfriends. Who would she choose? "Cleo," she decided.

Cleo took a deep breath. No way did mummies give up their secrets that easily. "Scare," she chose.

Frankie bit her lip, thinking. What was the funniest "scare" she could think of? "You have to kiss Webby!"

Cleo groaned. Webby giggled and puckered up his tiny lips. He gave a happy little trill. Disgusted, Cleo picked him up and gave him a quick peck. Webby fell over, swooning with delight and making gurgling noises. All the ghouls burst out laughing.

Draculaura jumped in. "Clawdeen, you're next. Truth or Scare?"

Clawdeen stared at Webby. Yikes! She didn't want to have to do something worse than kiss a pet spider. "Um, I'm gonna go with truth," she decided.

Draculaura clapped. "I know! What's your biggest dream? What do you want to do when we don't have to hide from the humans?"

Clawdeen held her pillow closer, thinking. Did she dare tell everyone? She had to! That was the game. "When I was a werepup," she told the others, "we lived in a dark, dingy den. There was no style, no art. But then Monster High found me. And I discovered how good it made me feel to be creative and to create for others too."

Clawdeen held up her sketch pad. In addition to her fashion designs, it was filled with the most wonderful watercolors about life at Monster High! But there were also drawings of a beautiful glass building filled with models wearing the latest styles. This was Clawdeen's vision. That's what she was always working on.

"So my dream is to open a salon," she continued. "A place for everybody. Humans and monsters alike. And I want to be the head stylist that makes them all say...*aroooo!*" She howled like the weregirl she was.

Wow! Her ghoulfriends applauded her vision and her honesty.

"Clawdeen, that's a spooktacular idea," said Frankie. "You should do it."

Clawdeen blushed. "Yeah, maybe someday."

"Or right now!" Draculaura had an idea!

"Now? What, like *now* now?" Clawdeen didn't understand.

Draculaura's eyes were sparkling with excitement. "Think about it. Opening a salon for monster style is the perfect next step to revealing ourselves to humans. We could all work there and get to know them, and they'll just think we're in costume."

"She's right!" Cleo agreed. As a royal princess, she spent a lot of time getting her hair done. "Nothing makes someone open up like sitting in a salon chair."

"But ghouls…" Clawdeen protested. "Where would the salon even go?"

A flash of lightning lit up the sky. It gave Frankie an amazing idea. "I know! The abandoned power station where I used to hide. It's the perfect spot for such a voltageous idea."

Clawdeen was overwhelmed. "This is all happening so fast. What if I'm not ready?"

"You're ready!" all the ghouls said at the same time. It was true. She was. Didn't she already have a sketchbook full of fashion and hair designs? She looked down at her pictures and thought about all the time she'd spent dreaming of her own salon. It was what she really wanted, wasn't it?

"Okay, let's do this," agreed Clawdeen, taking a deep breath. "Let's turn the power station into a fierce salon."

The ghouls cheered and waved their arms. Everyone hugged Clawdeen. They placed their hands one over the other and took a vow together. They were going to do this. Making Clawdeen's dream come true was a way to help monsters everywhere!

The lightning flashed again, but no one saw the pale face of a Zomboy peering in through the skylight. He'd heard everything. He groaned.

Chapter 7

LIGHTBULB MOMENTS

The lights flickered on and off at the abandoned power station, but no one noticed. And no one heard the sound of chain saws and electric drills from within. The noise of the storm and the flashes of lightning kept what was happening there a total secret.

"Those ghouls are coming here?"

A Zomboy, dripping wet with rain, stood in front of Moanica. He mumbled and grunted.

"To turn this power station into a salon?" Moanica fumed. Her hands were scrunched into tight fists.

"Uh-huh," confirmed the Zomboy,

his mouth flopping open.

Other Zomboyz were hurrying here and there, giant pieces of equipment in their outstretched arms. They were tinkering with generators. They were unraveling huge bolts of wire. They were sticking metal objects into plugs and shocking themselves over and over again…which was okay, because they were zombies.

"Ugh." Moanica sighed. "I'm kind of in the middle of a pretty outstanding scheme here." She gestured behind her. A Zomboy was up on a ladder hitting a pipe with a hammer. Another was dangling from a ledge by his hands, about to fall.

The Zomboy groaned apologetically.

"No, it's not your fault," said Moanica, holding her head in her hands. "We'll think of something." Which she did in less than a second. She turned to her minions. "Pack it up, Zomboyz! We're moving this party underground. Where zombies belong." She let out an evil cackle and stormed out of the power station, slamming the door behind her.

By the time the sun had risen, all signs of her work with the Zomboyz had disappeared.

It was a new day.

The sun was out and the birds were chirping when Frankie brought her friends to check out the location for Clawdeen's salon. She opened the doors triumphantly.

Cleo looked at the vast space filled with old, broken equipment. "*Hmmm*," she said uncertainly.

Draculaura wasn't convinced it was a good choice, either.

"It looks nice." Lagoona tried to be optimistic. Some broken equipment fell beside her. "It looks like I should be wearing a hard hat."

"I know, I know," agreed Frankie. "It may not look like much now." Still, she loved this old place. She'd spent a lot of time here before she came to Monster High, dreaming about having friends... and now she did.

"It's perfect," Cleo interrupted her. She had been walking around examining the space like a director. "I can see it now. Reclining lounge coffins in the waiting area here, a row of styling chairs with crystal skulls over there. And in that corner—wait for it—fog machines!"

Cleo unraveled a long bandage from her arm and began using it as a measuring tape. She stared at the large generator box, but the moment she touched it, sparks flew out of it. She ducked as a huge jolt of electricity shot across the room. It just missed Lagoona.

Cleo pointed at the glowing generator. "We should probably do something about that."

"It's going to take a lot of work to get this place ready," agreed Draculaura. "You sure you can do it, Cleo?"

"My family built towering pyramids that have stood for eons. Trust me: I can do this." The ghouls had never seen her so excited.

Clawdeen wasn't worried about the space, but she *was* anxious about the hairstyles and fashions that she was designing. She couldn't think about anything else.

When they arrived back at Monster High, Clawdeen was already panicking. She went straight back to the art studio, where she spent her every free moment. She'd pinned sketches all over the bulletin board, and there were bolts of fabric on the tables. Sketches were strewn across the floor. She had cut out patterns, and there were bits of clothing draped over various mannequins.

"No, no, no, no, *no*," she muttered to herself. She was unhappy with everything. She crumpled up a sketch she'd been working on. She pinned a ribbon to a dress on a mannequin. It looked terrible. She groaned. "Wrong. All wrong." She dumped a trash can over the mannequin's head.

She started drawing again, but soon she got frustrated and slammed her hand against the easel…and it fell over. Like a domino, it knocked over everything in the studio—the other easels, the chairs, the mannequins.

It was just too much pressure! How was she going to impress the humans? Everything depended on that. "I can't do this!" she cried out.

"Everything okay in here, sweet pup?" It was her mother, checking up on her.

Clawdeen sighed. "I'm designing looks for the salon's big opening night. But nothing is good enough!"

Mrs. Wolf picked up a long strip of green fabric that was hanging off one of the mannequins. "What about this one? This is good."

"Mom! That's just a sleeve!"

"Well, it's a very nice sleeve," she reassured

Clawdeen before patting it back into place.

Clawdeen groaned. "You don't understand. When we open for the Normies, everything has to be incredible. What if nobody likes what I do?"

Clawdeen plopped down on a pile of discarded wigs. She was completely discouraged. Mrs. Wolf settled in beside her daughter. She tried to comfort her. "Clawdeen, being creative is hard. You have to open up your heart and show it to all the world. Painful, yes. But joyful too."

Tears welled up in Clawdeen's eyes.

"I believe in you," continued her mother. "You just need to believe in you too. You can't rush great art." She wrapped her arm around her daughter and gave her a warm hug.

"You're right," said Clawdeen. "I have all the time in the world to get these looks perfect." She was putting too much pressure on herself. It was true.

Ari poked her head into the studio. She was holding up her iCoffin with a smile. "Hey, Clawdeen," she said cheerfully. "Question: is it all right if I tell some of my old Normie bandmates about the salon?"

"Of course, Ari," Clawdeen answered cheerfully.

"Great!" Ari was relieved. "And…is it okay if they post about it online?"

"Sure," agreed Clawdeen. "I mean, we want a lot of Normies to come to the salon."

"Okay, good!" Ari beamed happily. "Because all of that already happened. And now my fans are posting about it. And more fans are reposting it. Again and again…and again!" Her iCoffin lit up. She glanced at it. "*Ooh!* Again!"

Clawdeen gulped, trying to stay calm. "So…you are saying that…"

"We're going to have hundreds and hundreds of Normies at the salon opening this weekend!" Ari clapped her hands, delighted.

"Right." Clawdeen took a deep breath. "Hundreds of Normies. This weekend. Wait—*this* weekend?"

"Yeah," confirmed Ari. "Everyone was so excited, and then I got excited, and, well…" Her voice trailed off. She shrugged apologetically.

Clawdeen turned to her mother. So much for all the time in the world to make great art. "Now can I panic?"

"Officially, as your mother, I'm supposed to say no, but, yes, I would probably panic."

Clawdeen howled at the top of her lungs! *"AROOO!"*

But only for a few seconds. She didn't have any time to be upset. She raced around the studio picking up fabric. She straightened the mannequins. She picked up the easels. She took a big breath, and then she slapped a piece of paper onto a new easel and started sketching like crazy. After all, she had to get to work. The opening of her dream salon was in just a few days!

Chapter 8

ZAPPED!

Twyla was keeping a careful eye on Moanica and the Zomboyz. She was at her locker putting away her books when she spotted a couple of Zomboyz. They were carrying shovels in their hands and maneuvering a wheelbarrow through the hallways. They were all dirty and dusty and wearing mining helmets. The Zomboyz were definitely up to something! Twyla ducked behind a corner, and without anyone noticing, she snapped a photo of them with her iCoffin.

In science class, Twyla noticed another Zomboy piling wires and batteries into a box.

Another one was studying Frankie and taking notes while she worked on her battery project. There was even a Zomboy up in the rafters, disconnecting electrical coils. One long wire got wrapped around him, and he flew through the air like a trapeze artist. *Click. Click. Click.* Twyla took photos of everything.

That afternoon when classes were over, she followed a Zomboy outside. Twyla covered herself with a gray shroud and kept to the shadows, undercover. She had to figure out what was going on. Far away from the school, far away from the human town, far away from *everything*, a group of Zomboyz was standing behind a table covered with pastries, cupcakes, and desserts. Could the Zomboyz really be holding a bake sale? In the middle of nowhere? Why?

Twyla pulled out her iCoffin and called Frankie. "We need to talk," she whispered.

The wind was howling, and the rain was coming down hard. After a brief let-up, the storm was in full swing again. The ghouls met in the gazebo on the outskirts of the school grounds so that no one would overhear them. Lightning flashed in the sky.

Frankie carefully swiped through Twyla's photos. "Wow. This is good work." But what did it all mean? "Digging tools, Tesla coils, electrical equipment..."

Twyla held up a zom-brownie. "And who has a zombie bake sale in the middle of nowhere?"

Frankie's eyes lit up when she saw the baked goods. "*Ooh!* Brownies!" She opened her mouth to take a big bite.

"Don't eat that," warned Twyla. "I checked. It's, like, 90 percent dirt."

"*Eww.*" Frankie let it fall to the ground with a scrunched-up frown. "What could they possibly be up to? I feel terrible asking, but could you keep watching them?"

"It's what I do best," Twyla said, smiling. She faded into the shadows and vanished on the spot. A second later, she reappeared. She really was the daughter of the Boogey Man.

"Just please be careful," Frankie begged. "I don't want you to end up in any kind of danger."

Just then, a huge gust of wind whirled past the gazebo—and lifted off its roof! The storm was getting worse. Branches and boards clattered down all around them. "Whoa!" yelled the ghouls.

"You know, like now, for instance," gasped Frankie.

Lightning struck! Thunder boomed!

"Let's go!" shouted Twyla above the roar.

Together they ran toward the school through sheets of driving rain. The sky was exploding with lightning. Huge bolts were striking all around them. They raced toward the stairs, but just before they reached the front door, Twyla tripped and fell.

"Twyla!" Frankie turned toward her friend.

"I'm okay...I..."

But Frankie knew that she wasn't. She saw the lightning bolt the second before it hit—headed straight for Twyla. Frankie dove toward Twyla, covering her body protectively with her own. The lightning hit Frankie, blasting through her neck bolts. Frankie glowed. But she had been created during a lightning storm, after all, and she could absorb all that electricity. When she stood up, she was fine—and Twyla was safe. She blinked. Absolutely fine. Twyla couldn't believe it.

When they were inside, Frankie checked her neck bolts. They were a little loose, and she gently tightened them. All better.

"You saved me, Frankie. Thank you," said Twyla.

"Don't mention it."

Frankie was stretching as if she were sore after a workout. Her body gave a little twitch. She made a frizzing noise.

"Are you okay?" Twyla asked.

"*Wooh!*" Frankie shook it off. "I'm all right. A little lightning never hurt anybody. I mean, never hurt a Stein, anyway. But from now on, what do you say we meet indoors?"

Twyla laughed and gave herself a shake. She was so relieved that Frankie had saved her and that they were both okay!

A nearby light buzzed and flickered. A frazzle of electricity arced from the light...right into Frankie. She felt her bolts again, confused.

"Huh. That's never happened before."

"That was a lot of lightning out there," noted Twyla. "You sure you don't need some help?"

"I'm fine," said Frankie, not at all worried. "Listen, we're having another ghouls' night tonight, upstairs. You want to come?"

Twyla shook her head. "I think I've already had more excitement than I can handle. Thanks, though."

"Okay, well, if you change your mind, you've got my number."

Frankie headed up the stairs. She didn't realize that with her every step, electricity from all different light fixtures jolted toward her. She walked past a lantern and, *zap*, it blinked out. Its chain creaked as it swung back and forth. She walked by a chandelier and, *fritz*, every electric candle dimmed. What was going on? She felt kind of strange. Another bolt of electricity blasted into her shoe. She shook it off. Oh well. She'd probably be fine in a little bit.

Zap! Zap! Frizzle! Zap!

It was almost as if all the electricity in Monster High was attracted to Frankie Stein.

Chapter 9

GOING WITH THE FLOW

The ghouls were all sound asleep in the loft. Outside, the storm was finally quieting down. There was no more thunder and lightning. The rain fell softly against the windowpanes. The ghouls were lost in dreams. Cleo muttered in her sleep. Lagoona's breath made a quiet whisper like the surf flowing in and out. Webby rocked back and forth in his hammock made of cobwebs. Frankie glowed.

But Clawdeen was wide awake.

She could not fall asleep. She could not stop thinking about the opening of her salon. She had to come up with a theme.

She threw off her blankets and stepped over the sleeping ghouls. She snuck past Cleo, who was talking in her sleep. "I would look fabulous in these jewels, Mr. Talking Pineapple."

The whole school was dark and quiet. It was the perfect time to think. Clawdeen settled down in front of her desk, pulled out her sketchbook, and started to draw.

"What are you doing'?" asked a sleepy voice.

Clawdeen jumped, startled. It was Draculaura, sitting up in her bed and rubbing her eyes. Clawdeen's desk light must have woken her.

"I'm trying to work on our looks. But I'm not happy with any of my designs. We've really got to wow the Normies."

"Well…" Draculaura yawned, her eyes barely open. "Why don't you just bring monster style to the humans?" Then, she lay back down and rolled over, fast asleep again.

Clawdeen thought about what Draculaura had said. *Monster style? Monster style!* "That's it!" Clawdeen exclaimed, her eyes wide with excitement.

"*Shhh!*" whispered Webby.

Clawdeen grinned. She had the answer to her problem. She'd show Normies just how spooktacular it was to look like a monster! She was finally inspired.

As Clawdeen sketched away, the light on her desk sparked. A thin trickle of energy wafted through the air—right to Frankie. Her eyelids fluttered. She glowed a little brighter. How much more electricity could she handle?

The next morning, the storm was gone, but all the lights in Monster High were flickering—especially when Frankie walked by. It was as if she were an electricity magnet.

Twyla noticed the lights flickering as she walked to class. When Twyla saw Frankie, she was worried. She kept touching the bolts on her neck and twitching.

"Good morning," Frankie called out to her brightly. "That was quite a storm last night, huh?"

"Yeah," agreed Twyla. "That electricity thing is still happening to you?"

"It's no big deal." Frankie shrugged off her concern. "In fact, I woke up full of energy. Ha!"

Twyla tried to smile. "Right…"

The two stepped outside together. Shingles

had blown off the roof, trees were down, and debris was scattered across the campus. Still, students were out on the steps enjoying the sunshine—and getting in some last-minute studying before class.

In a hushed voice so no one would overhear them, Twyla told Frankie her plans. "So I'm going to spy on that Zombake sale. I'm pretty sure those guys are hiding something."

"Be sure to call me when you find out," whispered Frankie.

"I will."

Frankie looked up at the sky. Not a cloud in it! The mountains that surrounded Monster High were fresh and green after all the rain. The sun felt warm on her face. She just had so much energy today!

She spotted Dracula high up on the side of the building taking down the boards he'd nailed over the windows. Clawdeen's mom was watching him.

"Are you sure you know what you are doing?" Mrs. Wolf called up to Dracula.

"I can promise you that I'm not going to fall this time," he responded confidently.

Mrs. Wolf shook her head. "Because the way you're leaning…"

Dracula was holding on to the window with one hand and balancing precariously on the ledge.

He dismissed her worries. "It's all a matter of balance and…*AAAAAAH!*" The board he was holding pulled away from the window frame… and so did Dracula. His hands waved in the air helplessly. He slipped off the ledge and plummeted toward the ground. Down, down, down. But luckily, Clawdeen's mom was right there again—and, just like the time before, she caught him in her arms.

"Did you do that on purpose again?" she asked, raising an eyebrow.

"Yes?" Dracula answered. He tried to maintain his cool and turned himself back into a bat. It took him a few flutters of his wings to lift off the ground. Clawdeen's mom laughed, her hands on her hips. He flew back up to the ledge to continue taking the boards off the windows. She shook her head. He would probably fall again—and she would be right there to catch him.

But at least the storm was over.

Chapter 10

ALTERNATING CURRENTS

No one was buying any treats at the Zombake sale. No one even knew about it, except for Twyla. Still, two Zomboyz were manning the table as if a crowd might show up at any minute, only there was no reason why anyone should. They weren't advertising it, that was for sure. Another Zomboy appeared—only he wasn't bringing another tray of brownies or cookies; he was carrying a huge bundle of wires over his head.

The other two Zomboyz looked from side to side to check that the coast was clear. When they were sure that no one else was around, they gave each other the thumbs-up.

Carefully, they pulled back the bake sale table—
and hidden underneath it was a trapdoor! They
lifted the door, and the Zomboy with the wires
disappeared underground. They put the table
back in place. They were hiding a secret entrance.
But where did it lead?

Twyla was watching everything from behind a
tree. She had to find a way to get a look inside that
trapdoor. But how?

Off in the distance, she heard a slurping,
burping noise. It was Gob! Maybe he'd heard
about the baked goods or smelled them, and he
couldn't resist. Twyla whistled to get his attention.
He stopped, and she waved him over. She needed
his help with a plan! She whispered a set of
directions in his ear. He nodded, making little
gurgling noises.

Grinning, Gob ambled over to the table of
treats. His googly eyes darted back and forth.
He started pointing at the baked goods—the
cupcakes, the turnovers, the muffins—as if it
were really hard to make a decision about what to
buy. Then, strangely, Gob pointed at the school
and began burbling a stream of nonsense. He

was making all kinds of weird noises and waving his hands. Whatever it was, it sounded really important! It sounded like an emergency.

The Zomboyz glanced toward the school, just for a second. But that's when Gob sprang into action. He grabbed all the goodies into his arms—and ran away surprisingly fast, headed back to Monster High. Both the Zomboyz instantly took chase. And that was Twyla's plan. They left the entrance to the secret passageway unguarded.

Twyla waited until they were far away and slunk over to the table. Where did this secret passage lead? Using all her strength, she pushed away the heavy table and lifted the trapdoor. She gulped. The underground tunnel looked really, really deep. Carefully, she descended a metal ladder into the darkness. Dim lanterns were hung along the dirt walls. Her footsteps echoed in the passageway. It was creepy, but Twyla was determined. She wanted to help her new friends.

Tracks led along the tunnel, and the ground was strewn with shovels and wire cables. After she had gone a long way, the walls were no longer dirt but a strange crystal. They shimmered in the darkness. She could hear clanging and digging up ahead. Somewhere in the distance, Zomboyz were muttering to one another as they walked.

Twyla hugged the shadows as she came around the corner. She didn't want anyone to see or hear her. Two Zomboyz, wearing hard hats and carrying pickaxes, strode past her. She held her breath. That was close—but they hadn't noticed her. *Phew!*

But just ahead were two more Zomboyz guarding an entryway. They held crossed shovels in front of themselves like spears. How could she get them to leave? She had an idea. But could it really be that easy? Would it work? It was worth a try—after all, they weren't very smart. Doing her best to imitate the low, faltering voice of a Zomboy, she called out, "Hey guys! The Creepeteria has *brains* for lunch today!"

"Brains?"

"Brains?"

"Brains!" exclaimed both the Zomboyz, jumping up and down with excitement. In an instant, they dropped their shovels and raced down the tunnel toward the exit. They didn't see

Twyla blending into the wall.

Twyla peeked into the chamber they had been guarding. It was filled with Zomboyz digging with shovels and pickaxes. The walls were iridescent and glowing. One of the Zomboyz was piling glowing stones into a wheelbarrow. Twyla also noticed electrical equipment everywhere—coils and wires and batteries. Her eyes widened when she saw Frankie's science project. What was it doing here?

Across the chamber, she spotted Moanica with her hands on her hips. She was directing all this activity. "Get back to work," she was telling one of the Zomboyz. "You can sleep when you're dead. Or...well, you know what I mean. No more breaks until all the electricity up there is in there!" She pointed from the ceiling to Frankie's tiny project!

What was she going to do with Frankie's project?

Twyla took a ton of photos with her iCoffin—of generators, electrical sockets, and the wires hooked up to the battery. She stayed in the shadows, but every time the camera flashed, she risked getting caught. Luckily, Moanica thought it was just Zomboyz making electrical mistakes.

As soon as she had thoroughly documented the strange chamber, Twyla hurried back through the tunnel as fast as she could. She had to tell Frankie what she'd seen. She burst out the trapdoor—and ran right into two Zomboyz!

Meanwhile, in the power station, Cleo was busy turning an old factory into a high-fashion salon. Clawdeen's little brothers were scampering back and forth with equipment and tools. One werekid was hammering a wall panel into place while another was screwing lightbulbs into a beautiful bone chandelier.

Cleo marched among the chaos, happy to be in charge. "Come on, ghouls!" she encouraged them. She answered her iCoffin, nodding as she listened. "I don't care what your boss said, Rene," she answered, "that price is outrageous for cuticle scrapers!"

A few werekids dashed by, an outstretched mummy in their arms.

"Hey, be careful with that!" shouted Cleo. "Aunt Nephythis hates to be woken up."

Cleo turned back to the conversation on her

iCoffin. "Rene, I wasn't born yesterday. I was born six thousand years ago." She paused, listening. "Don't worry about how that's possible—worry about my cuticles!"

Lagoona came into the factory with a box of styling equipment. "Hey, mate, where do these go?" she asked Cleo.

"Oh, just over by the hair dryers for now," said Cleo. She glanced across the room and her eyes landed on a couple of the werekids messing around with the dryers. "Hey, hey, *heel*!" she ordered the pups. "That is not a toy."

The pup lifted up the dome of the dryer. He'd given his brother a Mohawk!

Frankie was over in the corner by herself. She'd been calling Twyla again and again, but all she got was her voice mail. *Hi, this is Twyla. Please leave a message.*

"Come on, Twyla, why aren't you answering?" Frankie was worried about her. What had she found out?

Frankie twitched. Some leftover electricity from the old generator behind her had flowed into her. She rubbed her neck bolt. It tingled. But other than that, all she noticed was that she felt a little more energetic. She had to find Twyla!

"Hey, Cleo," she said to her friend. "I'm sorry. I know we have a lot going on here, but I have to step out for a few."

"Everything all right, Frankie?" worried Cleo. She handed one of the werekids a paint roller. Frankie shrugged. "It's nothing I can't handle on my own. I just need to check on somebody." *Zap! Tingle! Zap!* Another jolt of electricity had found her.

"Do whatever you need to do," Cleo reassured her distractedly. Messages were pouring into her iCoffin. There were so many last-minute details to take care of before the opening of the salon.

"Lagoona and I will be fine over here. We have everything under control."

A werekid hanging on to some decorations on the ceiling swung past Cleo.

"Excuse me." Cleo took off after him.

Frankie shuddered. More electricity was pouring into her. It was everywhere in the old power station. Her eyes widened and she twitched again. Where was Twyla?

Chapter 11

UNPLUGGED!

The very first Monster High band was preparing for their very first practice. The group gathered in the school's courtyard. Rayth was fiddling with his electric guitar. Deuce took a seat behind his drum set. Woolee pinged her triangle. Venus shook a gourd and rocked her guitar. Skelly was on bass, and Bonesy strummed his keytar. Silvi tested out her microphone. She was going to sing backup with Venus. The band was ready to rock!

"Welcome to the very first jam session of Rayth and the Silent Screams," announced Rayth. "And a one, and a two—"

"Wait!" Deuce interrupted, his drumsticks poised in midair. The snakes of his hair hissed. "Hold up. We're not calling the band Rayth and the Something Something. Skelly said we were gonna be The Rolling Bones." He let loose with a triumphant drum solo.

Skelly and Bonesy gave each other a skeletal fist bump and rattled their finger bones in a secret handshake. *The Rolling Bones! Best. Name. Ever!* Their skulls spun round and round on their neck bones happily.

But Venus was frowning and wrinkling her nose with distaste. "We should name the band something more powerful. What about Thunder and Frightening!" She strummed a power chord on her guitar.

"No!" exclaimed Rayth instantly. "I like Rayth and the Silent Screams. Now let's jam."

Deuce shook his head. No way was he ready to start practicing. "*Ugggh!* You can't just name the band after yourself, Rayth."

"One, I'm the lead singer," explained Rayth. "Two, it's an awesome name, and three, let's jam!"

But nobody started playing.

Venus was thinking. "What about Ghoulish Intentions?" she suggested.

"*Oooh!*" squealed Rayth with mock enthusiasm. He narrowed his eyes stubbornly. "What about Rayth and the Silent Screams?"

Everyone started arguing. Woolee didn't know what to say. Silvi was getting fed up. This was no fun.

"It's traditional to name the band after the lead singer!" Rayth stomped his foot.

"That's the worst name in the history of names!" Venus protested.

Silvi pouted. She didn't like all this arguing. Without even realizing it, she transformed into a snarling wolf. Everyone stopped and stared at her.

"Whoa!" gasped Rayth.

She quickly morphed back into a ghoul and smoothed her hair. She took a big breath, trying to calm herself down. They were all taking this too seriously. "Look, I'm still the new ghoul here, but I know this isn't what Monster High is about."

Rayth and Deuce looked down guiltily.

"We didn't start this band to argue over something as silly as a name," Silvi continued.

"We're here to make awesome music together. Monster music." She let loose with a wild jam on her guitar. She was good!

The friends bowed their heads, ashamed.

"Silvi is right," agreed Venus. "We shouldn't be fighting like this."

Rayth kicked at the floor. "I'm sorry," he admitted.

"No, my bad," said Deuce.

Woolee nodded her furry head.

"Besides," added Silvi, "the band should be called The Howling Army." She let loose with a wild wolf howl. *"Awooo!"*

Woolee laughed. She pinged her triangle. That was a great idea. But nobody else felt the same.

"No!"

"No way!"

"Come on," Silvi pleaded.

"Trust me," fumed Venus. "I know what I'm talking about." The ghouls glared at each other.

Nobody could agree about anything! It was absolute chaos.

Frankie Stein builds a super battery.
Voltageous!

Clawdeen Wolf can't wait to open her own monster style salon!

Her ghoulfriends transform the powe station into the Fierce Salon.

Clawdeen is nervous, but her mom makes her feel better.

nwhile, Moanica and her Zomboyz
re working on a shocking plan...

While protecting Twyla, Frankie is struck by lightning and becomes supercharged!

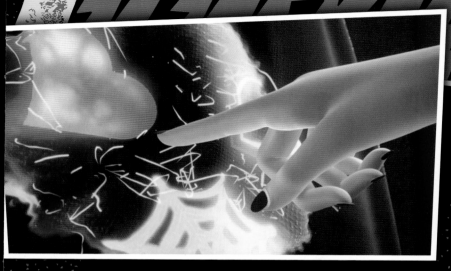

Frankie electrifies Clawdeen's clawesome designs!

Frankie creates Znap with
her extra electricity.

Twyla finds out Moanica wants to use Frankie's super battery to steal the Normies' electricity... but she needs Frankie to make it work!

The ghouls stop Moanica
and save the day!
The Fierce Salon is a success!

Chapter 12

SHOCKED AND AWED!

Clawdeen was finally ready to reveal her monster style designs to her ghoulfriends. They'd all come together in the art studio. They crowded around a giant display hidden under a tarp. Everyone had her eyes shut, waiting for the big moment.

"No peeking," said Clawdeen nervously. "Okay, ghouls. Here goes!"

Clawdeen took a big breath and whipped off the tarp. Beneath it was an array of mannequins, each one dressed in a spooktacular style. Flared skirts, lightning-bolt collars, bat-wing sleeves, and stylish belts.

"Creeperific!" gushed Draculaura.

"You are so talented," Ari complimented her.

"You really like them?" Clawdeen was smiling, pleased.

Draculaura nodded. "I can't wait to wear these at the salon opening tonight. They are fangtastic!" Draculaura was touching the fabric of one dress, impressed.

"Thanks." Clawdeen blushed. She exhaled at last. She'd done it. "All my inspiration was thanks to you and the ghouls. But I still think there is *something* missing…"

Frankie burst into the room, late, carrying an armful of notebooks and books. She was charging around in circles, unable to stand still, and talking a mile a minute as if she'd just drank four extra-strong Mummy Mochas. "Hey, sorry I'm late, but I just got this big burst of energy, so I decided to take a walk around the school fourteen times, you know, after I did the Humanology reading assignment…" She threw all the books in her arms up in the air.

"Who broke Frankie?" Clawdeen whispered to Draculaura, worried. Something was clearly the matter with her. But what?

Frankie fritzed and fizzled, a bundle of sizzling energy. She kept on talking without even pausing for a breath. "Oh, and then I did the rest of the reading for the next two semesters." Her eyes widened when she spotted the mannequins. "Oh! Those looks are so voltageous! I knew you could do it! Hey, do I sound like I'm talking fast? I'm talking fast, aren't I?"

Frankie was so jittery that she was pacing back and forth while she talked. Her arms were flinging this way and that, and she bumped into one of the mannequins and knocked it over. Little sparks were exploding all around her.

"Um, Frankie?" called Ari, trying to catch her attention.

"Frankie! Frankie, slow down!" Draculaura said to her friend. She rushed over to her. "How many Mummy Mochas did you drink?"

But Frankie was so hyper she could barely take in her friends' words. "Why? I've never been so full of energy! That's a great idea! I'll go get us all some Mummy Mochas. I'll be right back!"

Clawdeen reached out a hand to stop her. *Zap!*

Frankie electrocuted her!

"Whoa!" Clawdeen exclaimed. "No, no, no, why don't we sit down for a minute?" She guided Frankie over to a chair, making sure not to touch her again. The others gathered around, concerned.

Frankie was shaking and twitching. Her arms flailed uncontrollably. Her eyes were wide and unfocused.

Ari shook her head. "It's like there's too much electricity inside her. She's all amped up."

Frankie's hand brushed against one of the dresses! *Zap!*

"Oh no! My dress!" exclaimed Clawdeen. All her hard work! What had Frankie's electricity done? Was it ruined?

Absolutely not!

The place that Frankie had touched sizzled and sparked. The threads began to glitter and glow! The dress was electrified, and it looked fangtastic!

Frankie didn't even hear the other ghouls speaking. She placed her hands on another dress, and once again glowing streaks of shimmering energy spread across it.

"Oh my!" gushed Ari.

"Amazing!" agreed Draculaura.

Clawdeen was stunned. *"Ahoo!"* she howled. "This is what my outfits were missing! A power-station salon deserves electric fashion!"

The ghouls grinned, but Frankie just looked down at her hands. She had no idea what was happening. Bright streams of electricity were jumping between her fingertips! She touched another dress. Zowie! It lit up. She grazed her fingers over an outfit and it sparkled. Soon every dress was electrified!

Clawdeen was thrilled. Now she really was almost ready for the opening. All she needed was a fashion show run-through—for their classmates. Lagoona turned up the music and the ghouls started getting ready. Clawdeen would make a last-minute fix to an outfit, and Frankie would electrify it! After a break for Mummy Mochas, the ghouls picked out the dresses they were going to model and helped style one another's hair.

In the main hallway, the lights dimmed dramatically. Students stopped at their lockers, looking around.

"What's going on?" monsters wondered.

A beam of light fell on Ari, standing at the top of the stairs. "Presenting Miss Clawdeen Wolf's Fierce Electric Fashions!"

"Oh cool!"

"Hey, look!"

"A show?"

"A show!"

The ghouls made their entrance wearing Clawdeen's voltageous fashions.

"Look at those ghouls!" Silvi loved the new line of clothes!

Venus clapped her hands. "Bright lights meets frights!"

"Shock and awesome!" exclaimed Silvi.

The ghouls strutted down the steps, stopping now and then like models on the runway.

Ghouls rushed up to Clawdeen, wanting to know how they could wear one of these clawesome styles.

"Oh my gosh, oh my gosh! Can I get one? Can I get one?"

"We are really turning some heads!" Ari was so happy Clawdeen's outfits were a success!

The band had broken off fighting with one another long enough to see what was going on inside the school. Bonesy and Skelly's skulls spun around. Wow!

"Sweet!" said Deuce. His snakes hissed.

They couldn't believe what Clawdeen had come up with—especially Rayth, who had a crush on her.

"Hey, Cl-Clawdeen," he stammered. "You look, um—I mean you and the ghouls are, like, um—you are very…" He scratched his hair nervously. "Hey!" he added, holding up his guitar. "Did I mention we started a band?"

Clawdeen blushed. "Thank you, Rayth."

The ghouls passed through the crowd, their high heels clicking on the marble floors. They made their way to a classroom to take a break from all the excitement. The fashion run-through had been a success, but now they had to get ready for the opening itself.

Frankie was looking a little paler than usual. She'd lost some electricity making the dresses shimmer, but she still didn't feel like herself.

"Are you okay?" asked Draculaura.

"It still feels like there's a little electricity left. Maybe I can…" She shook her hands as if they had fallen asleep and she was trying to wake them up. She shook them harder. Tiny sparks flew out of her fingertips. She shook them even harder, and a giant ball of energy shot out of her hand and rocketed around the room.

The shining orb was literally bouncing off the walls! It ricocheted off the window. The ghouls ducked down to avoid getting hit by it as it flew past them. Wherever it hit, it left a black char mark.

"Look out!" called Clawdeen.

The ghouls dove out of the way. The ball crashed right where they had been standing—and created a huge smoking crater in the middle of the hall.

The ghouls were coughing and rubbing their eyes.

"*Zzzzznap!*" A tiny face poked out of the crater. He was bright yellow with spikes of blue and yellow hair and wide electric-blue eyes.

"*Awwww!*" gushed the ghouls.

"Adorbs!" said Draculaura, looking at the tiny

round creature with giant eyes and little ears. "What is it?'

"*Zzzznap!*" it said again.

Frankie giggled. "I guess it's a 'znap'!"

"*Znap! Znap!*" The little creature jumped up and down.

Clawdeen reached down to shake its little paw. "Well, it's very nice to meet you, Znap." She jumped backward. He had shocked her! "Maybe we can just bow?" she suggested.

Znap floated through the air right toward Frankie. He floated around her, studying her. She looked at him. He landed on her arm with a fireworks display of sparks. Frankie's hair stood straight up! She laughed, delighted. She didn't mind getting a little shocked.

"So, ghouls," Ari said. "Now that we have our fierce new looks, what do you say we head over to the power station and see if Cleo's ready for tonight?"

Frankie took out her iCoffin to see if she had any messages. She frowned. Why hadn't she heard from Twyla? "Let me catch up with you," she said to the others. "I have to check on something first."

Frankie took off out the front door before her friends could protest. For a moment, Znap hesitated. Should he stay or should he go? He looked at Frankie. He didn't ever want to be apart from her, and he buzzed through the air right after her devotedly. Wherever she went, he would follow!

Chapter 13

SHORT-CIRCUITED

Frankie went to the gazebo, looking for Twyla. But nobody was there. Frankie took out her iCoffin again. No messages. She called Twyla's number again.

"Come on, Twyla, where are you?" she fretted. "Something's just not right…"

Znap looked on worriedly as the phone rang and rang.

Little did they know that Twyla's iCoffin was lying on the floor of an underground chamber. It buzzed and glowed. Moanica picked it up and answered, "Wrong number." She clicked it off, dropped it, and stomped on the phone until it broke into pieces.

She cackled wickedly. Behind bars, Twyla watched her. Moanica had locked her up—and there was no way she could tell Frankie what was happening. Every time she touched the bars, they shocked her.

Moanica turned back to the huge electrical device the Zomboyz had constructed. Wires of all different colors coiled in and out of large metal plates. At its base was Frankie's science project.

"Are you still fiddling with that thing?" Moanica scolded a Zomboy who was trying to shove a three-pronged plug into a two-pronged socket. "I thought you'd be done by now."

A Zomboy rushed over and clamped a giant cable to the device.

"Well? Is it finished? Can we get started?" Moanica demanded to know.

The Zomboy held up a finger as if to say, *One second*. He studied the device. He took out a hammer and whacked at a bolt. A jolt of electricity flew into him and sent him flying across the room.

He groaned. He gave Moanica the thumbs-up.

"Finally." Moanica sighed impatiently. She shoved aside another Zomboy to get to the main control panel. She grabbed ahold of a giant switch.

"I know what you're up to!" shouted Twyla, trying to stop her. "You're stealing all the electricity."

Moanica raised a single arched eyebrow. "Oh really?"

"I figured it out," said Twyla. "I mean, we're underneath the power station."

Since the Zomboyz had captured and imprisoned her, Twyla had been observing everything around her. She'd seen how the wires went up to an electrical grid on the ceiling. She'd heard the thumping of music high above her. Behind all the noises of the Zomboyz working were *other* noises—doors opening and shutting, trucks making deliveries, the laughter of monsters working hard together. They were building the salon. But no one knew Twyla was locked up right beneath them. How would they ever find her?

Cleo was busily directing the last-minute finishing touches before the opening. Werepups ran here and there, boxes held in their teeth. Clawdeen arranged a display of clawsome fashion accessories. Ari hung a painting. Draculaura moved a plant to a better location. Lagoona set up the DJ station. The music had to be perfect for the big opening night. Cleo took a last look around. She polished a mirror. That was it. They were ready. The ghouls cheered.

Far below, underground, Twyla heard them.

Somehow, she had to stall Moanica. She had to keep her from going through with her plan. "You're going to use Frankie's science project to take all the electricity out of the power grid," she told her.

"Huh. And they say Frankie is the ghoul with all the brains," Moanica admitted.

Every Zomboy in the room froze. They dropped their shovels and their pickaxes. *Brains? Where?*

Moanica glared at them. "No, there aren't any brains."

Disappointed, the Zomboyz went back to work.

Twyla wasn't going to let Moanica get away with this! "You can steal the electricity to ruin the big salon opening, but it won't stop those ghouls from following their dream."

Moanica's eyes widened. She smiled. She laughed, flipping her hair over her shoulder. Twyla had not figured out her plan after all. "Oh, I don't care about their little salon or their misguided dream. Ruining that is just a bonus."

Excited, she hurried over to the device, proud of her evil plan. After all, she hadn't had anyone to explain her project to, except the Zomboyz, and they didn't really count.

"Professor Dracula said that Normies are afraid of the dark, right?" she said. "So when we use this bad boy to take all their electricity…total darkness! And when the Normies are good and scared, the Zomboyz and I will go out into the world and show them how truly scarifying we monsters can be. Right, Zomboyz?"

But she didn't realize the Zomboyz were taking a tea break. One Zomboy looked up from pouring a cup for another. Another one was dunking his cookie into his drink.

"Hey! Be scary!" ordered Moanica.

The Zomboyz held out their arms and moaned.

They were still holding their tea cups. They didn't look very scary, but Moanica was satisfied.

"This is the Night of the Zomboyz!" She cackled triumphantly. The time had come. She was ready at last! She threw the switch on the giant device.

The electrical wires buzzed. The room lit up. The crystal walls were glowing brighter and brighter. Electricity was pouring into the underground chamber.

Moanica examined Frankie's tiny project. There was a needle on it measuring input. It was moving higher and higher and higher like a thermometer. She clapped her hands. This was better than she had ever imagined—

Boom! A huge explosion filled the room and sent Moanica flying backward. Sparks flew! The machine smoked. It whirred to a stop. Frankie's battery was a puddle of melted plastic. Moanica's hair was frazzled.

"Impressive…fail," said Twyla.

Moanica was furious. "WHAT WAS THAT? I THOUGHT YOU ZOMBOYZ SAID YOU KNEW WHAT YOU WERE DOING!"

The Zomboyz shrugged. One of them took a sip of tea thoughtfully.

Moanica threw up her hands in frustration. "Worthless. I've gotta get some air. Time to think of a plan B."

Aboveground, one of the Zomboyz at the bake sale took a bite of a brownie. Not bad, but not as good as brains. Before he could sample one of the cupcakes, the trapdoor underneath the table flew open. Moanica stormed out of the tunnel in a total fury and headed to Monster High.

She blew in through the front door. Her hair was still electrified, and she was mumbling angrily to herself. Frankie was in the entryway, still looking everywhere for Twyla. Znap followed her wherever she went. He buzzed behind her.

Distracted, Moanica walked right into Frankie.

"Moanica?" she said. "You wouldn't happen to know where Twyla is..."

"Who, me?" Moanica answered defensively. "How should I know where that shadow ghoul likes to sneak?"

Her reaction made Frankie suspicious. "If you do know where Twyla is, I'll find out."

Znap nodded in agreement. He pointed his little finger at Moanica angrily. *"Znap, znap, znap!"*

When Frankie wasn't looking, Moanica made a face. *"I'll find out,"* she repeated mockingly.

But as she watched Frankie walk away, she noticed a thin stream of electricity zapping from an overhead light into one of Frankie's neck bolts. She passed another light and it happened again. *Zap!* What did it mean?

Moanica grinned wickedly. Frankie was a natural electricity magnet. This was better than she'd ever imagined. She didn't need Frankie's project to carry out her evil plan. She just needed Frankie!

Moanica pulled out her iCoffin. "Release the Boogey-girl," she ordered the Zomboy who answered.

He groaned in response.

"No, I'm not mad at you anymore." Moanica sighed. "You're still my Zomboyz."

Another groan came from the other end of the phone, but this one was more like a purr.

"Yes," said Moanica. She checked to make sure

no one was listening. "We can get ice cream after we finish the Night of the Zomboyz."

In the background, all the Zomboyz cheered—and they released Twyla.

Twyla ran as fast as she could through the tunnel. When she got to the trapdoor, a Zomboy shooed her outside. He snapped shut the door to the tunnel. What was going on? Why had they let her go? All Twyla knew was that she had to find Frankie.

Chapter 14

STATIC

The band was trying to practice again. After all, their big show was that night.

"All right, so it's settled," began Rayth. "The name of the band is Howling Thunder and Frightening Featuring Rayth and Deuce and the Rolling Bones…and Woolee."

Woolee gave him a furry thumbs-up.

Silvi shook her head, disappointed. "You know there's no way that's going to fit on a T-shirt."

"Hey," Rayth said quickly, trying to keep the peace. "Howling Thunder and Frightening Featuring Rayth and Deuce and the Rolling

Bones and Woolee isn't about T-shirts and making money." He placed his hand on his heart dramatically. "It's about our message and monster alternative." Rayth struck a chord on his guitar.

Deuce was just about to hit the drums when he paused, concerned. "Um. Monster alternative? I thought we were going to be playing heavy metal." He let loose on his drum set to make his point.

Rayth was stunned "No. *H-T-F-F-R-D-A-T-R-B and Woolee* is a monster alternative band—"

"Guys! Guys!" interrupted Venus. "Doesn't it make more sense for a monster band to play goth rock?"

Deuce threw up his hands. "Great, now we don't even agree on the kind of music we're gonna play? Bonesy, Skelly, what about you guys?"

Bonesy and Skelly exchanged a glance and began playing their instruments—the keytar and the bass. The easy sounds of smooth jazz filled the courtyard.

Everyone began arguing again.

"Only my mom likes smooth jazz!" Rayth said.

"Goth rock is totally now!" said Venus.

"Metal is the only cool music," added Deuce.

A blaring cacophony filled the courtyard as everyone played something different. It sounded terrible—and it was only a few hours until the opening.

Meanwhile, Frankie and Znap were still on the hunt for Twyla. Frankie was getting more and more worried. Something had to be the matter. She couldn't believe it when she heard footsteps— and saw Twyla running toward Monster High!

"Twyla!" she exclaimed.

"Znap!" said Znap excitedly.

Twyla was trying to catch her breath. She had run so fast.

"Twyla, where have you been?" asked Frankie. "I've been looking all over—"

"It's Moanica," Twyla interjected. "She had her Zomboyz dig a tunnel under the power station."

"Znap! Znap! Znap!" buzzed Znap. He waved and smiled. He couldn't wait to go to the power station!

Twyla stared at the tiny creature. "What's that?"

"I'll explain later," Frankie responded. She was too worried about this news. "Why on earth are they digging a tunnel?"

"Because she wants to steal all the electricity, all the light, so she can—"

Clawdeen interrupted her. "Frankie?" she asked. She was all dressed up for the big opening.

"Clawdeen? What are you doing here?" wondered Frankie.

"I came looking for you!" Clawdeen was exasperated. The salon was about to open and she needed all her best ghoulfriends there with her.

"Oh no, you shouldn't go back to the salon—" Twyla warned Clawdeen.

Frankie stopped her from telling Clawdeen. There was no need to frighten everyone…yet. "Clawdeen, your dream is becoming reality tonight. You go make sure everything is perfect. I'll meet you there soon."

"Okay," agreed Clawdeen. "But don't be late. Ah! I'm so excited. I can't stop howling. *Awooooooo!*"

As soon as she was gone, Frankie turned to Twyla. "Now, where is that tunnel?"

Together, the ghouls marched across the clearing with little Znap behind them. There weren't any Zomboyz at the pretend bake sale. All the treats were gone. The sign was torn down. It was completely abandoned.

"That's odd; they're usually here," Twyla noted.

Frankie couldn't see what the problem was. They just had to open the trapdoor. She and Znap tried to lift the table away, but Twyla stopped her.

"Frankie, I know you want to take care of this on your own, but listen. That cavern is swarming with Zomboyz."

"I am more than capable of outsmarting a few Zomboyz," Frankie said confidently.

"Znap! Znap!" added Znap in agreement.

"That salon means everything to Clawdeen," Frankie explained. "I'm not letting Moanica ruin her big night." She lifted up the trapdoor and began the climb down the ladder.

"Znap! Znap!" He did a somersault in the air and dove into the tunnel.

Twyla took a big breath. "Fine, then I'm coming with you." She headed back underground.

Frankie peered into the darkness. "So how far down does this go?"

"A long way," Twyla told her.

"It's really dark. Good thing I have my

own light source!" She fritzed and sparked, illuminating the passageway.

Znap floated before them, glowing.

What they didn't notice was the two Zomboyz grinning in the darkness behind them. Moanica had ordered them to let the ghouls pass by. The ghouls didn't know they were walking into a trap.

Chapter 15

A SIZZLING SUCCESS!

A huge crowd had gathered in front of the old power station. They were there for the opening! Music thumped from the salon. Lights twinkled around the door. Ari emerged from inside. She was wearing an electrified dress covered in musical notes. She looked fangtastic! The crowd went wild.

"It's Tash!" someone called. That was Ari's human name.

"Hey, she's got a monster makeover!"

"I love it!"

"I want one too!"

Ari had a microphone. "Hello, everyone!" she called out. "Thank you all for coming to our grand opening! I'd like to introduce Clawdeen Wolf, up-and-coming style genius."

Clawdeen was overwhelmed and a little nervous. This was her dream come true! "Welcome to...FIERCE!" she announced.

The doors were open, the lights were blazing, and the music was pounding.

The floor was covered in an intricate design. The styling chairs were monster chic. Neon signs blazed. A fog machine made the whole room eerily glamorous. The Fierce Salon was a happening scene. Ghouls strutted through the room in Clawdeen's fashions, lit up by Frankie's electric touch.

The Normies loved it all!

"Their monster makeup is so realistic!"

"Forget their makeup, did you see those outfits?"

"I'm telling all my friends about monster style!"

Cleo was styling a human's hair, giving her a monster makeover. It was wild! When the girl stood up, she looked at herself in the mirror, thrilled. Her friends clustered around.

"So cool!"

"Love it!"

"Fangtastic!"

"Fangtastic!" repeated her friend. They'd heard the ghouls using that word and loved it too!

Everyone wanted to look like a monster. They wanted the clothes, the hair…and they even wanted to talk just like monsters. Only they didn't know that monster style was the style of *real* monsters!

"*Ooh*, Mummy Mochas!" enthused a Normie. "Isn't that clever?"

Dracula was there—and he was letting his daughter give him a new hairstyle for the first time in, well, centuries. She buzzed up one whole side of his head.

"You're sure this looks good?" If only he could see himself in the mirror—but vampires couldn't.

"Absolutely," said Draculaura. "It makes you look at least ten thousand years younger!"

"I'm not so sure about that…"

"Love the new look," Mrs. Wolf complimented him. And after that, he decided his haircut might not be so bad after all.

"Well, what do you know? So do I!" he said.

Lagoona was spinning tracks and the Normies were dancing. Everyone was having a good time. But something was bothering Clawdeen. One thing was just not quite right. She gazed around the busy room. She was looking for something. Humans were running in and out of the changing rooms to try on new outfits.

"Check me out! I'm a monster!" someone said happily.

"You look creeperific!"

"I'm *so* coming here all the time!"

"Did you see they have a fog machine?"

Clawdeen checked her iCoffin. Nothing.

Mrs. Wolf wrapped an arm around her daughter. "I'm very proud of you, Clawdeen."

"Thanks, Mom."

But Mrs. Wolf noticed that Clawdeen wasn't perfectly happy. "What's wrong?"

"Frankie should be here," Clawdeen confided in her mother. "Just wondering where she is."

"I'm sure she's around here somewhere," her mother reassured her.

But Dracula interrupted them. In his arms and draped over his shoulders was a whole pack of werewolf pups—Clawdeen's little brothers. Mrs. Wolf smiled at her daughter again. It was time to get the little ones home. It had been a big night, a wonderful night.

If only Frankie could have seen Clawdeen's success.

Chapter 16

POWER FAILURE

Frankie and Twyla reached the entrance to the crystal chamber without seeing a single Zomboy. But Twyla warned Frankie that they were probably all inside.

"Seems pretty quiet," noted Frankie, looking around.

Still, Twyla was cautious. They entered the vast room as quietly as they could—but it was completely empty. No Zomboyz. No Moanica. They seemed to have packed up and moved out. The room was eerily silent except for a very faint thumping noise. It was the distant sound of the party far, far above them. Frankie spotted her science project. It was completely melted.

Znap made a sympathetic buzz when he saw how upset she was. Frankie rushed over to see what had happened to it.

"Frankie! Be careful!" exclaimed Twyla.

But it was too late. The Zomboyz were everywhere! They'd been hiding. They grabbed Twyla first.

"Znap! Znap!" yelled Znap helplessly as they put him in a glass jar.

Zomboyz lined the balcony above the room, peering down at them and groaning.

Moanica emerged from behind a wall of hanging wires. "So, Frankie, what do you think?"

"I think you ruined my science project!" Frankie replied.

"Oh…" Moanica laughed. "I'm about to ruin much more than that."

Frankie clutched her project. "I'm taking this whole thing apart before you can do any more damage."

"I don't think so." Moanica smiled confidently. "It's time for the Night of the Zomboyz. Time for the Normies to be afraid. And they will be, when I shut off all the lights!"

Moanica cheered with her arms over her head, and all the Zomboyz imitated her.

Frankie snorted with disbelief. "There are billions of watts of energy in that power grid. Obviously there was no way my project would be able to store that much electricity."

"Yeah, I kind of already figured that out, thanks. But that got me thinking. Where under earth would I find something, or someone, that *is* capable of absorbing that much electricity? *Hmmmm…*" Moanica cackled wickedly.

She waved her hands, and two Zomboyz crept up behind Frankie with jumper cables. But Frankie didn't see what was about to happen!

"You let Twyla go because you knew she'd lead me down here. You need me to make your machine work," Frankie realized.

"Yup," confirmed Moanica, a glint in her eye. She signaled the Zomboyz. "Now!"

Moanica pulled a lever. Sparks flew. Energy was pouring from the power-station grid right above them…directly into Frankie! Frankie's whole body was glowing. More and more electricity poured into her. What had been too much for Frankie's battery wasn't too much for her!

Moanica's plan was working! Now she had a way to steal all the electricity—and plunge the Normie town into terrifying darkness!

Chapter 17

TOTAL BLACKOUT!

The band was finally onstage! At last, they were ready to perform their first concert on the front steps of the school. Bright lights shone in their eyes.

Rayth stepped forward and grabbed the microphone. "Hello, Monster High! We are… Howling Thunder and Frightening Featuring Rayth and Deuce and the Rolling Bones and Woolee!"

Someone in the audience clapped and cheered. It was Gob. He was the only person in the audience. Everyone else was at the opening.

Deuce strummed his bass. "Who wants to hear some heavy-ish metal monster alternative goth rock with subtle undertones of smooth jazz?"

Woolee cleared her throat.

"And there's, uh, some polka in there too." Deuce sighed.

Woolee grinned and pinged her tiny triangle.

Rayth turned toward the band. "I said, a-one, a-two, a-one-two-three!" But no one moved. Rayth realized something terrible. "Hey, we never practiced any songs!"

"Yeah," said Silvi thoughtfully. "I was meaning to bring that up."

Out in the audience, Gob was eagerly waiting for the concert to begin.

"Uh—um—uh," stuttered Rayth. He thrummed a chord on his guitar. It wasn't tuned. It screeched with feedback.

Nobody else knew what to do. Woolee pinged her triangle.

Gob was starting to grumble when the lights suddenly flickered. For a moment, there was darkness, and then they came on again. Everyone was relieved. *Zap!* Electricity blasted through

the instruments...and disappeared. Electricity
flickered through the room...and disappeared.
It lit up Silvi's and Venus's dresses...and
disappeared. What was going on? Was this part of
the show?

"That's kind of cool!" exclaimed Silvi. Her
guitar was glowing!

"Nice!" Deuce nodded, pleased.

Even Woolee liked the effects. But Rayth felt
left out. "Where are my electric special effects?"
he grumbled.

A moment later, the lights went out for good.
Rayth tried to strum his guitar but there was
no noise. There were no lights. There was no
electricity.

It was all gone!

The lights were flickering in the salon.
Lagoona touched her turntable and was shocked.
The electric hair clippers stopped working.
The spotlights were on the fritz, sending mini–
lightning bolts across the room.

"What's going on?" people wondered.

In the Normie town, the same thing was
happening. First, the lights began to flicker, and

then they went off for good. There were no lights on in the houses. There were no streetlights. It was a total blackout!

Frankie was filling up with more and more electricity. Her hair was standing on end. Sparks were flying out of her fingers. Her skin glowed. Her body was rigid. Her eyes were wide and glittering.

In the Fierce Salon, the lights went out. Worried voices wondered when they were going to turn back on.

"What's happening?"

"Looks like a power surge," someone said authoritatively.

"I can't see anything!" a Normie yelled, setting off the panic.

Cleo tried to get everyone to calm down. "Um. Nothing to worry about, people! Just a little technical difficulty on our first night. If I could direct your attention to the table in the corner: Please help yourself to some refreshments."

Just at that moment, a power surge burst through the floor like a broken hydrant and blasted the table toward the ceiling.

"Okay, maybe hold off on the refreshments for the time being," said Cleo.

The Normies were freaking out.

"Should we leave?"

"It's getting kind of dangerous!"

"Yikes!"

Strange electrical noises—thrums and zaps and whirs—filled the room. Sparks landed on Cleo and she went electric. Sparks landed on Lagoona and she glowed.

In the secret underground chamber, Moanica was triumphant. She laughed gleefully as more and more electricity poured into Frankie. Frankie wafted back and forth like seaweed caught in a tidal current of pure electrical power.

The Zomboyz were holding on tight to Twyla. "Frankie!" called Twyla, trying to break free.

"She can't hear you!" Moanica cackled.

The glow coming from Frankie was blinding. How much more could she take? Slowly, Frankie lifted into the air, filled with power.

Twyla broke free from the Zomboyz, but she couldn't get to her friend. The electricity was like a shield blasting her backward.

The dial registering the amount of electricity in the room was climbing higher and higher. How much more could Frankie take?

House by house, street by street, town by town, country by country—all the lights were disappearing. All the electricity was disappearing…right into Frankie! The grid was down!

Bolts were busting loose. The dial on the register spun round and round. Frankie had broken it. She drifted toward the ground and dropped to her knees. Again, Twyla raced to her friend, but she could not touch her.

Moanica was victorious; she had done it. She had brought darkness to the world! Now it was time to release the Zomboyz!

Chapter 18

SCARED OF THE DARK

The whole world was dark—and it was quiet too. No electricity hummed through the power lines. The appliances weren't buzzing, the fans weren't whirring, no music was playing. In the salon, the only light came from the soft glow of the electrified dresses.

No one knew what to do. Everyone was still and waiting.

Until a Zomboy crashed through a trapdoor in the floor with a loud groan! More and more trapdoors were flung open. More and more red-eyed Zomboyz emerged from beneath the power station.

"Zomboyz?" cried Clawdeen.

The Normies began screaming.

Another Zomboy leaped onto the floor from below. An arm reached up. Another Zomboy was trying to haul himself upward, but he couldn't get the hang of it.

Moanica rose up on a giant platform, mighty and cackling! She towered above everyone.

The Normies backed away nervously.

Clawdeen shook her head. This was terrible. The salon opening was ruined!

"Moanica!" exclaimed Lagoona. What was going on?

Moanica grinned wickedly. "Boo! Are you scared?" she whispered dramatically. "Well, you should be! Monsters and zombies are *real*!"

The humans were in a panic.

"Zombies!"

"Help!"

"I didn't get my hair done yet!"

Moanica laughed at their fears. A thud interrupted her. It was one of the Zomboyz hauling himself up through the floor. But he was still stuck. He groaned and smiled.

"Will somebody please help him?" Moanica demanded as quietly as she could. She cleared her throat. She tried to make herself scary again. "And tonight under the cover of perpetual darkness, my Zomboyz and I are going out into your world. And we're going to do terrible, scarrible things!"

The Normies screamed and cried.

"That's right!" Moanica exclaimed. "We're gonna tie your shoelaces together! We're gonna put salt in your sugar bowls!" She struggled to think of the very scariest pranks she could. "We're gonna do a lot of things!" she finished. She raised her arms frighteningly.

"*Oooooooohhhh!*" groaned the Zomboyz, trying to be scary. They lunged toward the humans.

Screaming, the humans raced toward the door. They pushed one another out of the way. They couldn't get out of the salon fast enough.

"Ha-ha!" squealed Moanica gleefully. "That's right, run! Because this is the Night of the Zomboyz!"

"Moanica! What have you done?" Draculaura was so upset.

"I can't believe you would ruin this," cried Ari.

"Get back here right now!" Cleo told the humans. But no one listened to her.

Big tears welled up in Clawdeen's eyes. Her dream was ruined.

But Moanica had one more surprise to reveal. She stomped her foot—and the entire floor gave way! All the ghouls tumbled down, down, down underground! Now there was no way they could stop the Night of the Zomboyz.

The Zomboyz poured out of the old power station and began staggering toward town. They were ready for mischief! One started chewing on a mailbox. Another rang someone's doorbell over and over again, chuckling the whole time. Doors were locked. Curtains were pulled. Zomboyz hurled rolls of toilet paper over the power lines. They hid in Dumpsters and scared humans when they went to throw away the trash.

They banged together trash can lids and made frightening noises. They jumped up and down on parked cars and set off their alarms. They rolled garbage cans down the street. They laughed and groaned. Everyone was staying inside, terrified, while the Zomboyz rampaged.

Moanica surveyed the chaos happily. She'd wanted the Normies to be scared of monsters—and now they would be.

Chapter 19

JUICED

The ghouls rubbed their heads as they staggered to their feet. Where were they? They looked around at the glowing crystal chamber.

Dusting herself off, Cleo tried to be positive. "Well, if you don't count the whole zombies-stealing-the-electricity and falling-through-the-floor things, I'd say tonight went *pretty* well."

"Ghouls!" Twyla exclaimed, relieved. She ran over to them. "It's Frankie!'

"Frankie!" they all exclaimed.

At first they didn't even realize what they were looking at *was* Frankie. She pulsed and glowed like some star in a distant galaxy. She didn't seem to see anyone; it was as if she were in a trance.

"It was Moanica," Twyla explained tearfully. "She used Frankie for her plan."

"So. Much. Electricity," moaned Frankie.

"She's in shock!" said Cleo.

"We have to get all of that electricity out of her," Draculaura realized. But how?

"Znap! Znap! Znap!" Znap was buzzing inside a glass dome. Moanica had trapped him too. He wanted to get out.

Clawdeen had an idea. "Frankie. Whatever you did before to make Znap…can you do it again?"

Frankie's fingers moved ever so slightly, but no one was sure that she could hear them.

"Znap, can you wake her?" asked Ari, releasing the tiny creature.

"ZNAP!" he answered. He bounced toward Frankie. He nudged her arm. He nuzzled up close to her shoulder. He turned around and blasted her with a little jolt from his tail. He put his paws on her, and a tiny bit of electricity transferred to him. But it was enough. Sparks shot out of them both. Frankie's eyes fluttered. She stood up.

"Znap! ZNAP! Znap, znap, znap, ZNAP!" said
Znap excitedly.

Frankie's eyes opened, and she looked down
at her glowing hands. Sparks were flying out of
them. She struggled to stand up. She began to
shake her hands. She began to wave her arms.
They grew brighter and brighter! The light was
blinding!

"Hit the deck!" shouted Clawdeen, who realized
what was about to happen.

The ghouls ducked.

Pulsating balls of energy were flying out of
Frankie's fingertips. Hundreds of energy balls.
They were ricocheting off the glowing walls of the
crystal chamber. The room was filled with light
and color! It was like being at the very center of a
fireworks finale. Znap loved it!

One of them hit Twyla, and her whole
look went electric! Her skirt flared, her hair
was crimped, and her shoes were absolutely
voltageous.

Hundreds of balls were ping-ponging around
the room. When one hit the floor, it would
transform…into a znap!

Znaps with spiky hair were everywhere, happily buzzing together! They poured through the open ceiling up into the salon.

Frankie was transformed too. All the electricity had left her body—but her dress was electrified. It looked voltageous!

Everyone wanted to hug her at once.

"Hurray!"

"She's back!"

Frankie sighed. "I'm so glad that's over!"

"You're okay." Cleo was relieved.

"Thanks to Znap." Frankie laughed. "And you ghouls!" Frankie wrapped her arms around Twyla and gave her a hug.

Twyla was a little embarrassed by all the attention.

"You were right, Twyla," Frankie admitted. "I can't do everything on my own."

"*Znap! Znap! Znap!*" buzzed Znap.

Frankie picked up Znap. "You're right, Znap. With Moanica and the Zomboyz out scaring all the Normies, there's no way they'll ever trust us. Unless we do something."

"Moanica has hundreds of Zomboyz out

scaring those Normies." Clawdeen sighed. "It'd take an army to stop them."

Znap started jumping up and down, buzzing wildly. "*ZNAP!!!!*"

He had an idea. And it just might work.

Chapter 20

CHARGE!

The Normie neighborhood was covered in toilet paper and shaving cream. The Zomboyz were digging up flower beds and throwing around garbage. Everyone's yard was a disgusting mess.

Moanica dabbed at her eyes with a piece of toilet paper hanging from a tree. She was filled with happiness. "So proud," she whispered, watching her naughty Zomboyz run amok.

She grabbed a roll of toilet paper and threw it up over a lamppost. The lamp whirred. It flickered. It turned back on! How could that be? She had stolen all the electricity!

A Zomboy peering through binoculars started groaning. Warning! Warning!

Moanica looked down the street at an oncoming glow. Was it the sun rising? Was it some kind of strange rainbow? No, no, *no*! It couldn't be.

Moanica gasped. A row of electrified ghouls was marching toward her. What was happening?

"Hey, ghouls," she said. "Think you could turn the outfits down a bit? They're kinda messing up the whole dark and scary mood we've got going here."

Frankie stared at her defiantly. "Moanica, stop."

"We're not going to stand by and let you do this," Lagoona added.

Moanica sneered. "And you think a few shining, fabulously designed outfits are going to stop me?"

"Thank you?" Clawdeen replied. After all, a compliment was a compliment, even if it was from Moanica.

But Moanica was not interested in Clawdeen's gratitude. "Either grab a roll of toilet paper and help us decorate—or get out of the way.

Because nothing is going to stop the Night of the Zomboyz."

"Znap!"

"What is that?" Moanica whirled around toward the strange whirring noise. A Zomboy peered through two rolls of toilet paper like they were binoculars. He pointed at something small on the horizon.

Tiny Znap bobbed up the street. *"Znap!"*

This was it? This was all the ghouls had? Moanica burst out laughing. The Zomboyz chortled.

Znap barred his tiny teeth. *"Grrrr! Znap!"*

Frankie's eyes met Twyla's. They were waiting, listening. There it was! At first, they were just a distant hum. Then came a rising whir of sparks and zaps. Hundreds and hundreds of znaps were pouring into the neighborhood like a tidal wave!

Packs of znaps herded the Zomboyz out of town. They zapped their feet! They shocked their arms! They pushed them down the street!

A Zomboy swatted at a znap buzzing around his ears like a mosquito. Every time he tried to hit it, it zapped him. Zomboyz covered their ears;

they couldn't stand the high-pitched whirring noises that the znaps made.

Clawdeen turned into a wolf and howled with glee! *"Aroooooo!"*

Draculaura turned into a bat and started helping the znaps clean up the neighborhood.

Cleo began wrapping up Zomboyz with her bandages.

The znaps were buzzing along the electrical lines—and the lights were coming back on! Zomboyz were screeching and znaps were znapping. The Zomboyz waved their arms and jumped from leg to leg as if they were dancing. One Zomboy climbed a flagpole to get away from the buzzing orbs—and the znap sent a jolt of electricity up the pole. Shocked!

One Zomboy was trying to dig an escape tunnel. He dove in when it was deep enough... but a line of znaps followed him underground. One Zomboy hid behind a building, but Twyla emerged from the shadows and he ran away. Ari found another Zomboy hiding in a trash can and called over a couple of znaps. It was ghouls versus Zomboyz, and the ghouls were winning!

The Zomboyz were wrapped and frightened away.

Frankie had a little electricity left in her fingertips. She zapped one of the Zomboyz that had been left behind. "Thanks for making me part of your evil science project," she said.

Moanica grabbed a Zomboy and held him in front of her like a shield.

The znaps were driving off most of the Zomboyz. They were little, but they were fierce.

"*Znap! Znap! Znap!*"

"Have fun running away," Clawdeen called after them.

"See you at school on Monday," said Lagoona.

Moanica stomped her foot, furious. "*Oh, come on! Where do you think you're going? What about the Night of the Zomboyz?*"

Znap gave Moanica a little shock.

"Gah!" she screamed, overreacting.

A huge wave of znaps rolled toward Moanica and swept her off her feet. They dropped her right in front of the ghouls.

The znaps streamed up the telephone poles and zipped along the wires. The neighborhood began to hum and whir. Lights buzzed back on. Neighborhood by neighborhood, town by town, country by country—all the lights went back on.

"The znaps are lighting everything back up!" Draculaura clapped her hands.

"The power's returning!" exclaimed Ari.

Moanica pouted. "Terrific."

Znap gave Moanica one last zap.

"Hey! Stop that!" she told him. She looked to the ghouls for help, but they were just staring at her, their arms crossed. She slumped to the curb. She was defeated.

"You are in so much trouble," Draculaura said at last.

And she was.

The Night of the Zomboyz was officially over.

Chapter 21

POWER SAVERS

Dracula knew exactly what Moanica and the Zomboyz needed to do. The next day he got them to the salon to start cleaning up the mess they'd made.

"Okay, here we go," he said, handing Moanica a broom.

Dracula supervised as the Zomboyz squeegeed the mirrors and picked up debris with dustpans.

"Time for zom-beautification!" Dracula laughed at his pun. "Ha! Ha! Ha! Get it? Well, you know."

Znap was hovering over the Zomboyz, and any

time one of them stopped working, he'd give that one a little frizzle of a shock. *"Znap!"*

Dracula patted Znap on the head. "That's a good little…" *Znap!* He got shocked too. Ouch!

The ghouls were watching the Zomboyz and Moanica hard at work. They'd changed out of their electrified fashions into everyday clothes.

"Does anyone know how to say *That's what you get* in Zombie?" asked Lagoona.

All the ghouls giggled—except for Clawdeen. Lagoona realized she wasn't laughing and quickly apologized.

Clawdeen sighed and shrugged. She didn't feel like they'd won. "Nobody's gonna come back after that disaster last night."

"Maybe after the salon is fixed up, we could have another grand opening," Cleo suggested optimistically.

"Right!" agreed Ari. She was trying to be positive too. "Even better than before."

Clawdeen shook her head. "You ghouls are sweet, but let's face it. When those Zomboyz popped out of the ground, my dream was as dead as they are."

The ghouls hung their heads sadly. It was too true.

A few minutes later, the front door to the salon flew open. It was Twyla. "Ghouls! What are you doing just sitting around?"

"Trying to come up with a new dream for Clawdeen," answered Cleo. "What about something with music? There's a new band here at Monster High, and from what I understand, you do not have to be very good to get in."

Twyla looked impatient. "No. I mean, why aren't you getting ready?"

"Um, remember?" said Clawdeen. "Last night when the Zomboyz crashed the party?"

"I don't think I heard a single one of them compliment our decorations," added Draculaura.

A smile lit up Twyla's face. They didn't know! "Haven't you looked outside?"

The ghouls glanced at one another. What was she talking about? They rushed over to the window to peek out—and couldn't believe what they were seeing. There was a huge crowd of humans all waiting to get into the salon. More and more people were arriving every minute!

"Look at all the Normies!" exclaimed Lagoona.

Cleo couldn't understand it. "But Moanica... the Zomboyz..."

Twyla held up her iCoffin and flashed a news report. "Everyone thought that was all part of the opening," she explained. "They loved it! Your salon is trending all over the Internet. Monster style is officially the next big thing."

Clawdeen almost didn't dare to breathe. Could it be true?

"Well, what are we waiting for?" gushed Draculaura. "Let's get ready to meet the humans!"

"The dream is still alive!" Clawdeen had never been so happy.

"And it's going to be FIERCE!" said Frankie as she high-fived her ghoulfriends.

"*Whooo!*"

"Yeah!"

"Hooray!"

Even the Zomboyz joined in the cheering. After all, even zombies need a makeover now and then.